LOUELLA
and the
YELLOW
BALLOON

Molly Coxe

Thomas Y. Crowell   New York

Library of Congress Cataloging-in-Publication Data
Coxe, Molly.
    Louella and the yellow balloon.

    Summary: Patricia Pig takes her baby, Louella, to the
circus and loses her when Louella wanders off to
retrieve her new balloon.
    [1. Circus—Fiction.   2. Pigs—Fiction.   3. Animals—
Fiction] I. Title.
PZ7.C839424Lo 1988   [E]   87-30379
ISBN 0-690-04746-0
ISBN 0-690-04748-7 (lib. bdg.)

For
Mama, Daddy, and Tench,
and for Craig

Patricia Pig and her baby, Louella, were on their way to the circus.

5

They stopped to buy Louella a big, yellow balloon.
"Hold tight to the string," said Patricia.

6

Then they found their seats inside the big tent.
Patricia watched the crowd filing in to see the show.

When she turned back, Louella was gone.

Patricia searched under the seats.
Louella wasn't there.

Patricia climbed into the ring and asked
a performing bear, "Excuse me, have you seen
my baby, Louella Pig?"
"No, I haven't," said the bear.

Patricia asked a balancing mouse, "Have you seen my baby, Louella Pig?"
No luck.

So she asked the magician's rabbit,

17

a goose with a trained poodle,

a tamed lion,

and a troupe of acrobatic squirrels.

Not one of them had seen Louella.

Patricia was getting desperate. "Has anyone seen Louella Pig?" she cried.

Just then, she heard a commotion in the audience.
Everyone was pointing to something high overhead.
It was Louella! On the tightrope!

Patricia ran to the ladder and climbed up.
Louella lunged for her balloon.

She caught it, but lost her balance.
"MAMA!" screamed Louella.
She was going to fall!

And she would have. But Patricia was right
behind her.

She scooped Louella up and leapt to safety at the other end of the tightrope.

The crowd clapped and cheered and threw their hats into the air. Patricia kissed Louella and hugged her close. And Louella held tight to the string of her yellow balloon.